Please return or renew this item before the latest date shown below

East Mobile

Renewals can be made
by internet   www.onfife.com/fife-libraries
in person   at any library in Fife
by phone   03451 55 00 66

ON
AT FIFE
LIBRARIES

Thank you for using yo...

Barringto...   D1420030

First published in 2022 in Great Britain by
Barrington Stoke Ltd
18 Walker Street, Edinburgh, EH3 7LP

www.barringtonstoke.co.uk

A CIP catalogue record for this book is available
from the British Library upon request

ISBN: 978-1-80090-049-3

Printed by Hussar Books, Poland

For Lou

*Sometimes the only way to save yourself
is to save someone else ...*

Chapter 1

I'm told there is a mermaid in the millpond.

Not the sort of mermaid that sits on a rock, combing her pretty hair and singing to the moon. No, this mermaid is a monster – half-human, half-fish.

I'm told she has teeth like a pike and hands like a frog. And long webbed fingers that reach out of the water to catch animals that drink from the millpond at night.

I'm told she's so strong she can strangle a deer. Once it is dead, she drags it down into the water, sinks her sharp teeth into its neck and drinks its blood.

I don't believe a word of it of course – this tale the boss of the mill tells us. His horror story is meant to scare us workers into staying put. It is to make us too frightened to run away from the mill.

But the other children who came here with me from the London workhouse believe it. They are all hooked. They gawp and gulp at the tale like brainless fishes.

The boss and the gaffer show us around the cotton mill and explain what all the huge, noisy machines do. "You have to take care around the machines," the boss man says. "They can be very dangerous."

Then we're taken to the dormitory where we will be sleeping. There are twenty of us children in total. Me and eight others from London, and the rest who were already here.

My bed is right by the window, looking out over the millpond below. The view is better than the view from the workhouse window in London, all smoggy roofs and chimneys.

The cotton mill is in a valley, edged by thick green forest. When the machines fall silent, you can hear birds singing. Shallow streams trickle down from the hills into the millpond. Water is drawn off to turn the giant wheel that powers the mill. Beyond the mill, the water pushes against a dam, rushing through a narrow gap and down into the fast-flowing river. This, the boss man said, is called the weir. And it is very dangerous. Everything seems dangerous here.

The girl in the bed next to mine is small – only five or six perhaps. But then she looks up at me, and I see by her face that she is older than that. She's the same age as me probably – about eleven. I've seen children like her before – children who haven't grown because they've never had enough to eat. She holds her hand out and her thin face is one big beaming smile. "I'm Dot," she says.

"Bess," I reply. But I don't shake Dot's hand. "I'm not here to make friends," I say.

Dot shrugs, still smiling, and says, "None of us is here to make friends."

"Don't bother with Bess," Sam calls to Dot. Sam's one of the lads from London. He is on the other side of the dormitory, unpacking his small

bundle of clothes. "Bess don't talk to anyone much. Thinks she's above us."

I give Sam a long look, then turn back to the window.

"And don't ask what happened to her mother," Sam goes on. "Or you'll end up like me." Sam is laughing, and I know that he will be pointing to his missing front teeth. He's probably poking his pink tongue out of the gap I made in his teeth with my fist. The other children from London are all laughing too now.

"Bess turns nasty pretty quick," says one of them.

There is a scuffling noise. "Shut up about my ma!" another boy shrieks in a silly voice, pretending to be me. "Oof!" They are acting out the fight I had with Sam a few weeks ago back at the workhouse.

Dot waits until they have finished their stupid game. Then she whispers to me, "Did she die, Bess? Your ma?"

I nod. But I don't turn away from the window.

Chapter 2

"My ma was an actress," I murmur to Dot. "At Covent Garden Theatre. She was in Shakespeare plays and everything. The London papers said she was a rising star ..."

"Lawks!" Dot gasps. "Covent Garden! A rising star – your ma!" Then she says, "I never had a ma or a pa. The first thing I remember is being in the workhouse and then I came here to the mill."

Dot says it as a plain fact – not as if she feels sorry for herself or anything. But I still feel bad for her.

At least I have known what it is like to be loved – to be scooped up into a hug when I fell over. To be kissed on the forehead and tucked warmly into bed ... I can feel my heart reaching out to this lonely scrap of a girl, but then I snatch it back again.

Kindness won't get you anywhere, Bess, I say to myself. *You reach out to people and they just drag you down with them. That's all there is to it.*

I made a vow when Ma died and I was sent to the workhouse in London just a few weeks ago: *I am going to be as hard as nails. As tough as old boots.*

"I'm sorry, Dot," I say.

But I don't say what I'm sorry for ... *For you never having a ma or pa. For not wanting to be your friend ...*

I blink back the tears that are stinging my eyes and burning my throat. I clench my fists and take a long, shaking breath. I can almost feel my heart hardening in my chest again. It is a relief. This is how I feel safe now. Not caring about anyone. This is how I will survive. I'm on my own, and I need to make a plan ... There's no way I can stay here. As soon as I saw those machines and the thin, dead-eyed children working on them, I realised I'd made a big mistake leaving London.

"I won't be staying long," I say.

I hear the rustle of blankets as Dot curls up in her narrow bed, but I know she is still watching me. The other children are all quiet now. It will be an early start in the morning. We have to be up at five, the boss woman – the gaffer – said.

I gaze out at the millpond. The water is still.

"You looking for the mermaid, Bess?" Dot whispers.

"I don't believe in mermaids," I hiss in reply. But I can't help looking, and I can't help thinking about Ma – her last performance at the Covent Garden Theatre. It was Ma's biggest role so far – she was playing Ophelia in *Hamlet*. Ophelia is the beautiful young woman who drowns in a brook:

> *Her clothes spread wide and,*
> *mermaid-like, awhile they bore her up ...*
> *but long it could not be till that her*
> *garments, heavy with their drink, pull'd*
> *the poor wretch ... to muddy death ...*

It is almost dark now. Moonlight gleams on the glassy surface of the millpond. *What was that?* There was a twisting and churning in the water – and a glimpse of a huge grey, feathery fish-tail.

I stare and stare, squinting at the dark water.

But there is nothing there now.

Only a ripple that spreads out slowly and disappears.

Chapter 3

I first try to escape from the mill the next morning. It is very nearly a success.

It's all in the performance, Bess, I say to myself. I puff my chest out and stick my chin in the air. Then I walk straight out of the door as if I'm one of the bosses. I get halfway to the bridge before I feel a hand gripping my arm – as tight as a vice.

"You get back here!" Miss Tucker shouts.

After that, there is always someone watching. Miss Tucker is the gaffer in my part of the mill – she's in charge of the spinning room. Since I tried to escape, she follows me up and down the spinning machine, giving me a kick when I don't focus on the threads.

I am to work as a piecer here, like most of us who came from the London workhouse. It means I have to watch for when a thread snaps and fix it fast – before the great metal frame of the spinner comes clattering back towards me.

It is tricky at first. I have to spot the flickering threads, catch them and roll them back together again, often walking backwards at the same time. But I get the hang of it after a while. It is not hard work. The hardest thing about it is the heavy, humid air. The air is kept like that on purpose, to stop the cotton from drying out. But I feel as if I can hardly breathe. My head pounds with the heat, and with the roaring and banging of the machines.

Still, I think, *I'd rather do this than Dot's job*. Dot is a scavenger. It means she has to squirm about on the floor under the big clanking machine, gathering up all the fluff. Several times I catch my breath, thinking Dot is about to be crushed to death by the machine. But she always wriggles out of the way just in time, quick as a lizard.

"*Piecer!*" Miss Tucker bellows.

I've missed a thread. I spot it at last, catch the flying ends and rub them together as the machine spins and stretches the yarn. Miss Tucker is glaring at me. She's as big as an ogre. Her hands are huge and meaty.

"Wake up!" Miss Tucker yells. She strides over, towering above me. I look her right in the eye. I won't show her I'm afraid.

"You'd better not try running away again, Piecer," Miss Tucker snarls. "We *own* you, remember? You're under contract till you're twenty-one."

I scowl at her as she walks away,
swaggering with her own importance. The
worst thing is, she is right: they *do* own me.
I signed the contract myself.

The boss man from the mill visited the London workhouse to sign people up. I liked the idea of leaving London – a fresh start somewhere else, away from all the bad memories ... He told us we would sleep in feather beds, feast on roast beef and ride fine horses along the sparkling river here in the valley. But really it's all thin blankets, fleabites, cold porridge and tales of a monster mermaid.

I think of the grey fish-tail I spotted last night, sweeping through the dark water. Just a carp, I should think. I don't believe in mermaids. But there isn't much to do while I am waiting and pacing here at the spinning machine. So I choose to imagine the mermaid – a wild creature, half-child, half-fish, out there in the millpond ...

And it does not scare me at all. She's not a monster, just hungry. Just trying to stay alive, like the rest of us. *You have to be selfish to survive,* I think. *Selfish.* And my brain plays

with the word, still picturing the mermaid –
sel-fish ...

I imagine her swimming freely, floating,
turning and diving right down to the bottom of
the pond. She's skimming the stones, gliding
past the gentle weeds. I envy her. I want to feel
that cool deep water. My gaze drifts up to the
windows – tiny squares of yellow-green sunlight
that drip with condensation.

I can't stay here, I think. *I am an animal in
a cage – a creature in a cooking pot ... If I stay
here, I know I will die.*

"*Piecer!*" Miss Tucker bellows to me again.
And I drag my attention back to the monstrous
machine.

Chapter 4

At Ma's theatre, I would sometimes help out
backstage. I loved that excited tingling feeling
I had as we got ready for a performance –
knowing I was part of it all. I didn't care what
I was doing – sewing costumes, powdering wigs,
trimming candlewicks or sweeping the stage.
The hours always flew by. But here at the mill,
time drags so slowly I can hardly bear it.

A bell clangs loudly and I feel sure it must
be the end of the day – eleven hours gone by.
But it is only dinner-time. The machines grind
to a stop and we are all marched outside to use
the stinking privy. Then we go in to dinner

and gather around a woman who is giving out potatoes. Most of them look black and rotten.

Dot gets her potato before I do. It is dumped into her outstretched apron. The woman turns to the next child, but then Dot whips her potato into a skirt pocket. Her movement is so practised and fast it is almost invisible. Dot is still holding her apron out. Her face is blank, innocent.

"Sorry, ma'am, you missed me out," Dot says in a sweet voice.

And she is given another potato – a better one this time.

I am impressed.

*

The afternoon passes just as painfully as the morning – even more slowly perhaps. I catch the broken threads and rub them together, catch and rub them, catch and rub them ... I'm overwhelmed by heat and exhaustion. Sunlight is glaring in through the high windows. The spindles spin, the machine clanks and roars ... I find myself swaying on my sore feet, my eyes closing ...

"*Bess!*" It isn't Miss Tucker this time, it's Dot, saying, "*Fingers, Bess!*"

I snatch my hands back from the spindle, just before they get caught. My heart is thudding at being jolted back to reality. My fingers burn, imagining the crushing they so narrowly escaped. I am angry at myself for drifting off, angry that I nearly made such a terrible mistake.

"It's best to fix the threads when the machine is coming this way," Dot says.

"I know," I reply.

"If you wait till it's turning," Dot goes on, "you can get your fingers caught in the—"

"I *know!*" I snap. And for some reason my eyes start filling with tears. *"Don't help me!"*

Then there is another voice, screaming, *"Piecer! Scavenger!"*

We both turn around. Miss Tucker is striding this way.

"Bickering, eh?" she says. "Wasting time? Not on my watch, you filthy little guttersnipes. *Ungrateful*, that's what you are. Stupid and ungrateful. Need to be taught a lesson ..."

*

Dot and I are both beaten as a punishment.

The back of my legs swell up, turning as black as those rotten potatoes. Dot's skinny legs look like they might snap in two with each blow that comes. Yet she doesn't cry, and nor do I. I close myself up until I feel like I am hiding in a cupboard deep, deep inside myself. No one can hurt me here.

Chapter 5

Miss Tucker locks me and Dot in the dormitory after she has finished teaching us our lesson.

"I'm sorry," I say to Dot after Miss Tucker has stomped off down the stairs. "That was my fault. I shouldn't have shouted at you like that."

"I was only trying to help," Dot says.

"I don't need help," I say quietly. I try to swallow down the lump that is rising in my throat. "I don't need anyone."

Dot shrugs. "Fair enough." A grin twitches the corners of her mouth. "But you probably need your fingers."

I can't help but smile at that. Half-crying, half-laughing, I wipe my eyes on my sleeve. Dot offers me her grubby hanky and I take it.

"Not all mills are this bad," she says. "One of the boys in the weaving shed says he's heard of a mill in Manchester where they train you properly. They teach you to read and everything. You work half the day and then have school in the afternoons. They feed you well too."

"Manchester?" I sniff.

"Yep," Dot says.

"How far is that?"

"A few days' walking," Dot tells me. "A bit less if we went by barge. If we're lucky, we can catch a lift up the canal."

I think about it. "We could do that."

"We could."

We look at each other for a moment. I can feel a grin just like Dot's starting to spread across my face. *Are we making a plan together? A plan to escape?*

But then the heavy footsteps stomp back up the stairs. Miss Tucker fetches us and marches us back down to the mill. But this time she puts Dot to work in a different room.

*

The last hours I spend all alone at the spinning machine are far, far worse than the boredom I felt this morning. My legs shake beneath me – exhausted and throbbing with pain from being beaten. My fingers fumble the threads. The tears in my eyes mean I can barely see the whirling broken wisps.

At last, there is a sound – a bell. *It's over – thank goodness.*

We all drift into a messy line to leave the spinning room, but the machines keep

on going. An army of children walk past us –
pale, dead-eyed. They take our places at the
machines.

"Double shifts," a blond boy next to me
murmurs. "Must be a big order in. The
machines will be running through the night."

We all use the privy, wash and line up for
supper. I am looking for Dot, but I can't see her
anywhere. I haven't seen Dot since Miss Tucker
marched her off to work in another spinning
room. I hope she is all right.

"Have you seen Dot?" I hiss to the blond boy.

He looks around too. "Nope."

Sam is standing behind the boy. "Dot's so
little," he says. "Perhaps she fell right down the
privy."

I give Sam a shove.

"All right, Bess," he says. "Don't knock me other teeth out. Not just before supper anyway."

We sit down with our broth and bread, and hear a loud noise outside. A banging, rumbling sound.

Everyone looks up – has something happened? Has a building collapsed? Has the water wheel crashed down into the river?

Then rain starts lashing at the windows, and lightning flashes blinkingly bright. A storm is right overhead – *that* was the noise. The thunder crashes and rumbles again.

"Well," says the blond boy. "What with that and the machines all running, there won't be no peace and quiet for us tonight."

Chapter 6

The boy is right about the noise. The constant grumble of the machinery is like my poor tired brain turning over and over. The storm passes at last, leaving the air even hotter and more stifling than before. The dormitory is so airless and suffocating that we open all the windows.

London in the summer was bad – the rotten stink of the gutters, the fish market, the heavy stench of the Thames. I thought this place would be better, and maybe it is out in the green valley – but in here it is like an oven.

I lie awake for hours, even though I am exhausted. Every time I nearly fall asleep, I am woken again by the heat or the pain. My back aches badly from standing all day. The soles of my feet are blistered from the rough stone floor. My bruised legs are still throbbing.

Dot's bed is empty – she still has not returned. What can have happened to her? Is it possible Dot has escaped? Run off to Manchester without me?

I feel a wave of anger rush through me. Anger at Dot for disappearing without a word. Anger at myself too, for breaking my vow to be selfish. I had almost started to think of Dot as a friend ...

One of the smaller boys is crying at the other end of the dormitory. I could get up and see if he is all right ... But I don't.

If you're going to survive this, Bess, I say to myself firmly, *you can only think about yourself.*

You made yourself a promise. No one else matters. You've got to be as tough as old boots in a place like this. It's the only way to survive.

So I roll onto my side, turning my back to the boy's sobs and to Dot's empty bed. Eventually, I drift to sleep.

It doesn't take long for the nightmare to come. It's the same one that has haunted me nearly every night since Ma died. It creeps into my dreams, turning everything dark. It draws me back into the past, back into the wings of the Covent Garden Theatre.

And the nightmare is so real – the smell of freshly sawn wood, painted scenery and sweaty costumes. There's the waxy aroma of make-up. Chandeliers blaze above the stage. And there is my ma, standing all alone in the golden light. She is dressed as Ophelia, singing her last, sad song. Her eyes are dim, clouded. Ma looks so lost. My chest aches for her. I know what is going to happen next, and there is nothing I can do to stop it.

Ma's voice stutters. She cannot catch her breath. The audience murmurs with disapproval. Ma is shrinking away – smaller and smaller. She's the size of a child, the size of a mouse. I am terrified she will slip down the cracks between the boards. I run and catch Ma up, but I am too late – she is so tiny now I can't see her at all. I freeze, afraid I will tread on her. The stage lights blaze down, so very hot. I am all alone on the stage ...

I force my eyelids to open and stagger to my feet, dizzy and half-dreaming. I lean out of the window, gulping at the cooler air. But I still feel as if I am burning, unable to breathe. I lean further out. The millpond glimmers beneath me – black, shining, cold.

Jump, the water whispers.

Yes ...

I find myself sitting on the stone window ledge, reaching for the water with my toes. I twist around, lowering myself down until I am dangling. Then I plant my feet on the wall, push away and let go ...

Chapter 7

I am falling. *Flying!* There is a glorious moment of freedom as I wait for the deliciously cool water below. Then it hits me, as cold as a knife.

The shock of the water wakes me fully. I thrash to reach the surface and gasp at the air, treading water until my panic fades. At last, I am floating and calm. My nightclothes billow in the water around me. I laugh as I bob about like a jellyfish.

Ma taught me to swim in the Serpentine two summers ago. I am surprised at how easily the movements come back to me. I lie back, allowing the water to carry me. It cools my fevered brain and soothes my aching back, my bruised legs, my blistered feet.

The sky above is clear now. I can see stars – *so many stars!* They're like sugar dusted all over the black sky. The night never looked like this in London. I can still hear the machines of the mill, but the noise is softened and distant – like a train clattering on a faraway track.

I know I mustn't fall asleep, floating here, but the water is so cool, so soothing ...

There is a splosh and a swirl nearby. I twist around quickly, gulping in a mouthful of water. I splutter and struggle.

I feel another movement in the water – a cooler current swooshing past my legs.

Suddenly my heart is banging against my ribs.

It couldn't be ... Could it?

There's a dull splash – just a few yards away. I catch sight of a huge feather-grey tail.

I don't believe in mermaids, I tell myself. *I don't believe in mermaids.*

I try not to think about all the horrid things the boss man said – her needle-sharp teeth

and long frog-like fingers ... The water churns again. I can see the shadow of something beneath the water. Something huge and grey. *A fish*, I say to myself. *An eel*. But the thought of a giant eel is not helpful or comforting in the least.

I keep upright, facing it – whatever *it* is. My feet are limp in the water. I don't want to attract its attention. Every inch of my flesh is crawling with terror as I wait for pointed teeth and claws to touch me.

There is a roaring sound behind me. The noise blurs into my fear and the banging of my heart. It gets louder and louder until it drowns out everything else. And the water is tugging at me, sweeping me backwards …

The weir!

I strike out, pulling away from the fast flow of the water as it rushes towards the wall and crashes down into the river beyond. I kick, haul, scoop and thrash at the water, but it is no good. A fierce current is dragging me down. Water fills my nose, my throat. I gag on it, choking, fighting for air.

And then something happens.

I feel cold webbed fingers closing around my wrists. I struggle at first, but the fingers are pulling me out of the current, away from the roaring of the weir. They pull me right across the millpond, leading me to the grassy bank.

I grab the grass and splutter, coughing up great gobbets of water. At last, the air rushes back into my lungs. I breathe and breathe, clinging to handfuls of shaking grass. I can't let go of dry land. There is a splash and a strange gurgling sound right beside me.

Something is there. The thing that rescued me.

I don't want to look, but I know I must.

I turn around slowly.

Chapter 8

I blink and blink, my eyes streaming with water and tears as I hold tight to the bank of the millpond.

A creature is looking back at me. She's half submerged in the water – scrawny, strange, with wide bulging eyes. There are gaping gills on her neck, and she has grey scaled skin.

For a moment we just stare at each other. My mind scrabbles to try to make sense of what is happening. Is it possible I'm still dreaming? Still trapped in my nightmare?

I don't believe in mermaids, I think desperately. But the creature in front of me doesn't seem to care whether I believe in her or not.

She moves closer, closer. She tilts her strange head to one side as if she is trying to decide what to do with me. Is she going to kill me? *But she just rescued me ...* I think. Perhaps she wants to toy with me – like a cat with a mouse. Maybe she'll enjoy herself before she strangles me, and then she'll drain my blood.

Suddenly, I think about Dot. Is this what happened to her? Was she drawn into the water too? ... *Am I the mermaid's next victim?*

I don't wait to find out. I clamber up onto the bank. My numb limbs are shaking, my wet feet slipping on wet grass, scrabbling just out of her reach.

The mermaid lunges towards me, stretching out her thin grey arms. She opens her fish-like

mouth and makes the gurgling sound again.
I stare at her rows of dirty teeth, as sharp as
needles.

I wonder if she is going to chase me up onto
the bank. Can she climb out of the water? Move
on land?

But then there is a sound, and the mermaid
turns back to look at the mill. I look too and am
horrified to see the huge shape of Miss Tucker
striding over the bridge towards me.

There is a movement in the water, and I am shocked to realise the mermaid has vanished. Only a few circles ripple the dark water where she was just a moment before.

"*What on earth is going on out here?*" Miss Tucker bellows. "*Is that you over there, Piecer? Trying to escape again?*"

And before I can scramble to my feet, she has grabbed a handful of my hair.

*

The beating I get is worse than last time. Twice as many strikes. But somehow I feel it less than before. I think the cold water has numbed my legs. That and the shock of everything that just happened – half-drowning in a weir, being rescued and then attacked by a monstrous mermaid ...

It is dawn now. The others will all be eating their breakfast, getting ready for another day at the machines. I wonder if I will be allowed to go back to the dormitory, but Miss Tucker has other plans.

She marches me to an old stone warehouse attached to the farthest end of the mill building. Miss Tucker opens the door and shoves me inside. *"You'll stay in here today, Piecer!"* she bellows. *"Nothing to eat all day. Nothing till tomorrow morning. Maybe then you'll start behaving yourself."*

She slams and bolts the door, and it is suddenly completely dark.

I crouch down and feel about with my hands. I find something scratchy and softish that feels like a pile of old sacks. I sink down onto them, shivering in my soaked nightclothes. My stomach growls. A whole day in here with no food at all? What will I do?

Sleep, my body says.

And somehow, I actually do fall asleep, despite the hunger and the pain and the cold. It's almost instant – a deep, dreamless, exhausted sleep.

Chapter 9

When I wake up, it is warmer in the warehouse – much warmer. My nightclothes have almost dried out – they are all crispy and stuck to my skin. It must be another hot day out there. There's a narrow sliver of sunlight coming from the far wall of the warehouse. Dust motes float and dance in the air as if in a spotlight on a dark stage.

I follow the sunbeam across the room, trailing my fingers in its light, moving slowly so I don't trip over anything. At last, I reach the wall and can see the light is coming from behind a large bit of rotten boarding. I heave at it with all my might, pulling and pulling until the board splits, coming right away from the wall. It leaves behind just a few rotten bits of wood still attached to the rusty nails that once held the board in place.

Behind the board is a small broken window. Daylight floods in – filling the whole warehouse with summer light. Suddenly I can see where I have spent the hours of the morning – a great filthy room filled with broken bits of machinery, old furniture and rotten barrels. Rolls and rolls of mouldy cloth sit against the wall near the door – too spoiled to be sold. Everything here is covered in mould and dust and cobwebs.

I turn back to the window. It looks out over the millpond – the upper end of the pond where the water runs off to the flume that turns the mill's water wheel. The water is green and glassy in the sunlight, still and mysterious.

I can see a small fish darting about just below the surface – supple and silvery. A trout perhaps. It wafts its fins, drifting closer to me. The window is only a few feet above the water. I feel I could almost reach down and catch the fish with my fingers ... But then I see other fingers reaching for it – grey, scrawny, webbed fingers – and I almost scream.

The fingers grab the twisting fish, and the mermaid swims into view. Her strange fish eyes break the surface of the water. She opens her mouth and bites the head of the trout right off. Then she eats the rest of it quickly, while its body is still squirming, its tail still flapping. The mermaid crunches and chews. Fish blood and yellow juices run down her chin.

My hands are over my mouth to stop myself from gasping aloud. She is so close to me.

Does she know I'm here, watching her?

The mermaid answers me by turning around and looking me dead in the eye. Her face is smeared with fish guts. She opens

her mouth just as she did before and makes
that strange gurgling sound. Then she flips
backwards like a seal and swims in a great
circle around the pond. Faster and faster
she swims, always the same anti-clockwise
circle. She weaves around the rocks of the far
bank, dodges under the sucking water of the
weir, bashes her tail against the wall of the

warehouse. It is an odd thing to see – such a large creature swimming fast around such a small pond. It reminds me of a caged animal, or a falcon flying on a line, or a predator pacing in a pit ...

The mermaid is trapped, I realise suddenly. *She can't swim upstream because it is too shallow and rocky, and she can't get over the weir ...*

"We're the same, you and me," I whisper, and I press my hands to the dusty window. "Trapped. Alone ... Hopeless."

"Alone and hopeless? Speak for yourself!" a voice shouts. I jump nearly a foot in the air.

The voice didn't come from the mermaid beyond the window but from the far corner of the warehouse.

Someone else is in here with me.

Chapter 10

The rolls of cloth jiggle and shift, and a small figure crawls out.

"*Dot!*" I shout.

"Thought it was you," Dot says, beaming up at me. "Actually, when I first woke up, I thought it was rats or something moving about. But then I heard your voice. Who were you talking to?"

I can hardly say the mermaid ... "Nobody," I say instead. "Just thinking out loud. Talking to myself. What are you doing here, Dot? What happened to you?" She is touching the side of her head, inspecting her fingers for blood. "Did Miss Tucker put you in here?"

Dot nods, then winces.

"They found out I was nicking the potatoes. The cook told Miss Tucker yesterday afternoon, and I got another beating. Then the cook gave me a whammy around the head with a rolling pin, just for good measure."

"Oh, Dot ..." I say, going to her. I turn her head gently into the light so I can see. "There's a big old lump, Dot."

"Hmm," she says. "Think it must have made me go a bit funny. I don't remember much about being put in here. Think I've been out cold all night."

"All night and half the day," I say. "It must be afternoon now."

"No wonder I'm so hungry."

I laugh. "Me too," I say. "But I don't think we're getting out of here soon. Miss Tucker said not till tomorrow morning."

"Just as well I nicked this then ..." Dot says, and reaches into a pocket hidden by her threadbare shawl.

She pulls out two slices of bread and butter, all folded over and a bit squashed. "They took my potato, but they didn't get my extra bread and butter!" She passes one slice to me. "Sorry. Might be a bit warm and stale. Been in my pocket since breakfast yesterday."

"I don't care if the bread is mouldy and the butter is off," I say. "I'm so hungry." My mouth is already watering, despite the bashed look of yesterday's breakfast. "Thank you, Dot."

I take the bread gratefully and tear into it. It's only when I swallow the last bite that I realise I have crumbs down my front and butter on my chin.

Dot is watching me. She is nibbling her bread and butter as slowly and carefully as she can, making each mouthful last.

"Sorry," I say. I wipe my face on my sleeve and pick the crumbs off my nightgown.

"It's all right." Dot grins. "But that's all we've got till tomorrow morning. Unless ..."

"Unless what?" I ask.

"Unless we escape. Run away to Manchester like we said."

"But Miss Tucker bolted the door," I say. "And I'll never fit through that tiny window."

"Maybe not," Dot says, with a mouthful of bread and butter. She squints at the window. "But I reckon I would."

"We'd have to break the rest of the glass from the frame," I say, inspecting the window too. Then I look down. "And ... Can you swim?"

"Like a fish," Dot says, still grinning.

*

So we make a plan. We'll wait until it's dark. Dot will climb out of the window, swim to the edge of the millpond and drag herself up on the bank. Then she'll come around the side of the buildings to let me out of the warehouse.

If no one's about, we'll try to get some food from the kitchens. Then we'll set off. Dot says we need to head west until we find the canal. Then we follow that north towards Manchester – walking or on a barge.

"I've never been on a canal boat," I say, feeling a rush of excitement at the thought of our adventure. "Ma and I went on a pleasure boat on the Thames once. And last summer we hired a rowing boat on the Serpentine at Hyde Park. I nearly fell in." I find I am smiling at the memories.

Dot watches me carefully for a moment, then she says, "What happened to her? Your ma?"

I take a breath, and for some reason my eyes are drawn back to the tiny broken window.

I imagine Ma as Ophelia, with flowers in her hair. She's floating all pale and limp among the water weeds and lilies, out there in the millpond ...

I can hear the trickling of the river, the rushing of the weir, the splashing of the water wheel, the rumbling of the mill. But in this dusty old warehouse, with Dot, there is a sort of gentle stillness.

"My ma died of tuberculosis," I say quietly. "And it was all my fault."

Chapter 11

The boy outside the theatre was the thinnest, saddest little creature I had ever seen. He was always there by the stage door, every time Ma and I left the theatre at night. All on his own, in his ragged clothes. He watched us with his big round eyes as we passed him, wrapped up in our warm coats. Ma and I would usually be laughing together, holding gloved hands as we climbed up into the cab to go home.

When it snowed, I couldn't bear to ignore the boy any longer.

"I want to help him, Ma," I said.

So we asked him if he wanted to come home
with us.

"You can have a hot bath," I said. "Hot food."
The boy looked at me. "You'll be safe," I said.
"You can trust me."

So he came with us. He didn't say a word.

He stayed for three nights, sleeping on the floor by the fire – despite Ma making up a proper bed for him. The boy ate whatever we gave him, politely, gratefully. He had a bad cough. Ma gave him medicine and rubbed ointment on his thin little chest at night. I almost started to think of him as a little brother.

The boy didn't tell us his name. Didn't speak at all. We called him George, after the King, which he seemed to like. He even smiled once – when Ma gave him some clothes she'd found at the theatre. They were bits of old costumes that weren't needed any more. George looked as grand as you like – all clean and dressed up in a smart soldier-boy's jacket. But the day after that, he disappeared.

He was gone when we woke in the morning. Our front door was left standing open and some money had been taken from Ma's purse.

I was angry with George, but Ma wasn't. She was just sad that he had gone. She worried about him, looked for him on the streets every evening. But we never saw him again.

It was a few months later that Ma started getting ill. Pale and thin. She started coughing. The same cough as George had – racking and bloody. People say you get tuberculosis from poisoned air, but I know it was from that boy. I brought him into our home, and he poisoned it. He poisoned my ma ...

She couldn't perform any more – she was too weak. She coughed all the time and couldn't get through her lines. She lost her job. She got thinner and thinner – fading away right in front of me – and there was nothing I could do.

Ma told me to sell things so that we could pay the doctor and pay our rent to the landlady, Mrs Bridger. We sold expensive things at first – Ma's jewellery and furs, a few bits of silver. But

then the furniture. The plates. The coal scuttle.
Anything at all.

It was when I got home after selling my
best boots that Mrs Bridger met me at the door.
The doctor had been there – I saw his carriage
driving away up the road. Then Mrs Bridger
took hold of my arms and steered me up to her
flat. She gave me hot sweet tea. She told me
that Ma had died. She told me I couldn't stay
there if I couldn't pay the rent.

Mrs Bridger sent me to the workhouse the
next morning.

Chapter 12

Dot has not taken her eyes off me the whole time I've been telling the story.

Now that I'm finished, Dot gets up and comes to sit right next to me. She gives me her grubby hanky. She hugs me, and I let her.

I've been swallowing my sobs down as best I can, but now I can't bear the pain any longer. My sobs break like water over the weir, dammed up and held back for weeks and weeks. They spill over, free and crashing and released at last. I cry into Dot's neck, and she holds me tight. A few days ago, I would have hated her for such kindness. I would have hated myself too – for not being tough enough.

My heart hurts. It's been clenched tight for so long but is now letting go at last. It hurts so much to feel things again.

"It wasn't your fault your ma died," Dot says quietly. "And that little boy. He must have been so scared. Imagine what he must have seen in his life to make him run away even from kindness."

"Yes. I know," I say, and think of the small amount of money he stole from Ma's purse – only enough to buy a hot meal. And I think of Dot stealing the extra potatoes and bread from the cook …

"It wasn't that boy's fault your ma got ill," Dot went on. "It wasn't anyone's fault. You did the right thing to try to help him – to be kind."

Yes.

I think about the vow I made to myself – to be selfish, never to help others again … It was a vow I made when I was angry and grieving. There's a reason I've found it so hard to keep. *It's not in my nature to be like that. It doesn't feel right.*

I wipe my eyes on Dot's hanky and blow my nose loudly. We both laugh.

"About this plan of ours, Dot ..." I say. "Breaking out of this place. Going to Manchester ... Do you really think we can do it?"

"Of course I do," Dot says. "It won't be easy, but we can do it. We're as tough as old boots you and me."

And I smile again. "We'll wait till it's dark," I say.

And Dot nods.

"But there's something else we need to do before we go. Someone who needs our help," I tell her.

Dot raises her eyebrows.

I take her hand and lead her over to the window.

The millpond is as smooth as a mirror beneath us. It shows a perfect reflection of our two ghostly faces peering out through the frame of jagged glass. But then a shadow swims beneath the surface – huge and silvery grey.

Dot gasps as the mermaid's face breaks through the water just below us. The gills on her scaly neck are pulsing. She is looking at us with her big round fish eyes.

"Lawks!" Dot gasps.

Chapter 13

We spend the last hours of daylight unravelling
the great rolls of cloth that are stored here
in the warehouse. There are plenty of bits of
sharp metal lying around, and we cut off the
best bits of cotton – enough to wrap around
ourselves as skirts and aprons. After all, Dot
will be soaked and I'll still be in my nightdress
when we get out of here.

I choose a dark blue material with an
even darker apron. Dot chooses a bright
sunshine-yellow apron and rose-pink cotton
for the skirt beneath. She looks at our new
clothes – slightly moth-eaten, slightly mouldy.

"Very nice," she says. "Yours is more practical. But I like my colours better."

We find two long metal poles – rusty but still strong. We weave them through opposite sides of a long piece of thick cotton cloth to make a sort of stretcher. We are going to use this to rescue the mermaid. I have no idea if our ridiculous plan will work, but I know I have to try.

Then we wrap our hands and feet in strips of cloth and start snapping the last jagged shards of glass from the window frame so that Dot can slip out of it safely.

All the time my heart is thumping away – somewhere between joyful and terrified. The time goes so fast – just as it used to in the theatre when we were getting ready for a show.

"Do you think there's a Theatre Royal in Manchester, Dot?" I ask suddenly.

"I'd think so," Dot says. "Or some sort of theatre anyway. Bound to be. It's a big city."

I feel another flutter of excitement, thinking of a future even better than the millwork and schoolroom Dot has promised. *Perhaps the theatre might be interested in hiring an apprentice who trained at Covent Garden Theatre ...*

But I mustn't get ahead of myself. There are so many hurdles between here and there. So much that could still go wrong ...

*

When dusk falls, we begin our plan.

Dot takes off her threadbare shawl and skirt. I look at her skinny bruised legs, and I am more determined than ever for our plan to succeed. I'm going to help Dot put some flesh on those bones if it's the last thing I do.

She climbs carefully out of the window, head first. When she is clear of the frame, she dives downwards, hitting the water so cleanly it barely makes a sound. Dot surfaces a few feet away.

The mermaid is there, gliding and twisting and watching.

"She won't hurt me, will she?" Dot asks, suddenly looking pale.

And the truth is, I don't know.

"I don't think so," I whisper back. "I think she knows we want to help her." I look at the mermaid, and she looks right back at me. I try to hold her with my gaze. "We're the same, you and me," I whisper to her again. "And, tonight, we're both getting away from this place."

The mermaid stares a moment longer, then she duck-dives down into the weeds.

Dot is nearly at the bank now. She reaches it and scrambles out, and I find myself releasing a long, trembling breath.

Dot runs over the bridge and slinks silently along the shadowed warehouse wall. She darts around the corner and out of sight. Moments later I hear the bolt being drawn back from the warehouse door, and she is there – dripping and grinning. *My friend Dot.*

"Come on then," Dot says. I gather up all the things we have prepared, while she dries herself off and dresses in the new clothes we have made. I have already changed into my dark skirt and apron.

Dot grabs a big square of cloth we cut earlier. "Food," she says, and darts off into the shadows.

"Wait," I call softly, following her. "I'm coming with you."

"No point both of us risking our necks," she hisses. "I know my way around that kitchen blindfolded – and I'm small enough to fit through the bars of the back gate."

I nod, and I can't help smiling a bit. Dot is exactly the sort of brave and brilliant friend I need by my side for this adventure.

"Meet me by the weir," I say. And she does, just a few minutes later. The cloth square is now twisted into a heavy bundle. "Got a loaf of bread and a whole block of cheese!" she says delightedly.

"Well done!" I say. "Now for the really tricky bit."

And we both stare at the water.

Can we do this?

Chapter 14

The mermaid comes closer – slowly, cautiously.

We lower the stretcher we made into the shallow water, just opposite the weir. It's the same grassy bank Miss Tucker dragged me from last night. I was trying to escape from the mermaid then. Now, I am trying to help *her* to escape.

"It's all right," Dot says gently to the mermaid. "We won't hurt you."

The mermaid is hesitating, bobbing in the deeper water. Watching us. Watching the floating stretcher of cloth. To swim into something so much like a net must go against all her instincts.

"It's all right," I whisper too. "It's all right."

I keep looking up, scanning the dark buildings for movements. I am waiting for a door to open and close, and heavy striding footsteps coming to drag us back into the mill, throw us behind another locked door … We may never get another chance like this to escape, but I can't just go. I can't leave the mermaid here – trapped and alone.

Slowly, slowly, she gets closer. She touches the stretcher with the tips of her froggy fingers, then backs away.

It takes an age for the mermaid to come back again. An hour? More? The moon is high above us now. It's another clear warm night. Another sky kissed with a million stars. If ever there were a night for a miracle …

"You can trust me," I whisper. And I think, at last, she understands.

The mermaid swims closer and lifts herself onto the stretcher with her thin grey arms. She beats her strong tail in the water to push herself forward.

Now that she is so close, I am terrified. My heart thunders in my chest, and I can feel sweat running down my back.

The mermaid curls up her body until she is resting fully on the stretcher, then she looks up at me and bares her pointed teeth.

"Quickly, Dot," I say. "We need to do this quickly."

We lift the stretcher's metal poles. The material strains under the weight of the mermaid. She is surprisingly heavy. Her body is skin and bone, but her tail is thick and muscular.

I stagger backwards as I hold the poles, slipping slightly on the dewy grass. The mermaid jolts. She whips her head around and bites my arm.

I press my lips together to stop myself screaming. Somehow, I'm still gripping the metal poles of the stretcher.

"Stay still," Dot tells me under her breath. "Don't move."

Every muscle in my body is shuddering. At last, the mermaid releases my arm. Pinpricks of blood ooze up where her teeth punctured my skin. She twists into a ball, squirming on the stretcher like a captured snake.

"She's scared, Bess," Dot says. The gills on the mermaid's neck are gaping and closing frantically. "We need to get her into the water again."

Somehow, we manage to stagger all the way around the weir and down the bank to the open river that lies beyond. Dot and I fall to our knees at the water's edge and the mermaid flops herself off the stretcher and into the river.

Splash.

"We did it." Dot laughs, breathing hard.

"We did it!" I say.

We take a moment to catch our breath, watching the ripples fade on the water. *We did it*. Then we stand up, and I hoist the bundle of food onto my back.

"This way?" I say, nodding west.

"This way," Dot agrees.

Something jumps and sploshes in the river beside us. There's a silvery-grey shadow twisting and shimmering just beneath the surface. It weaves and darts about playfully. Then a powerful tail smashes the surface, and the shadow vanishes into the depths of the river.

She's free.

I look back at the mill – a dark ugly shape, towering over the valley. Then I turn to face the path. Moonlight dances on the river.

I have no idea what lies ahead of us. I have no idea where Dot and I will end up, or what the future may hold. But walking away from the darkness seems to be a good start.

Our books are tested
for children and young people by
children and young people.

Thanks to everyone who consulted on
a manuscript for their time and effort in
helping us to make our books better
for our readers.